Falling

CAT CLARKE

First published in 2013 in Great Britain by
Barrington Stoke Ltd
18 Walker Street, Edinburgh, EH3 7LP

www.barringtonstoke.co.uk

ISBN: 978-1-78112-207-5

Printed in China by Leo

For Caro, for falling in the best possible way

Chapter 1

You're not supposed to kiss someone who ISN'T your boyfriend. It's pretty much the first rule of relationships. But that's what I did last night. It was an accident. Well, it was *sort of* an accident. I feel bad about it now, of course. The guy wasn't even all that good at kissing.

My best friend Tilly keeps going on about it. She started the minute she arrived at my house to get ready for the party. I can tell she feels I've let her down, and she's the one person in my life I never want to let down. I kind of wish I hadn't told her, but she'd have known something was wrong. Tilly can *always* tell when I'm lying – not like Cam.

Tilly's sitting in front of the mirror in my room as she does her hair. It looks messy and cool, and extra red today because she dyed it last night. "I just don't understand why you would do it, Anna!" she says, for the 17th time. "AND the night before you're planning to ... you know." She puts on some eyeliner in one smooth sweep. I've never been able to master that.

"I *told* you, Till," I say. "I don't know why I did it! I just ... did. Can we change the subject? And could I maybe get some mirror time? I don't want us to be late. Cam's already annoyed that I wouldn't go help him set up for the party." This isn't exactly true. My boyfriend Cam does not get annoyed with me or anyone else – ever. That's part of the reason everyone loves him so much. Cameron Field. Mr Nice Guy. The most popular boy in our year by miles.

I adjust the straps on my bikini before I put my top on. The bikini is very tiny and very pink. Cam loves it. Cam loves everything I wear because he is the perfect boyfriend. He has perfect teeth, the perfect body and perfect manners when he speaks to my parents. They bloody love him. And his parents seem to love *me*. It's like they've all gone crazy and made up their minds that the two of us are going to get married one day or something.

The thought of getting married makes me want to scream. The thought of getting married to *Cam* makes me want to scream, bash my head against a wall and run in front of a truck. The weird thing is, I'm not even sure *why* I feel this way. And I can't tell anyone, because everyone thinks we're *perfect* together. Even Tilly. I guess that's why she's giving me such a hard time about that boy I pulled.

Tilly's right, of course. It's extra crappy to cheat on your boyfriend the night before you have sex for the first time. And tonight's the night. Cam insisted we wait for my 16th birthday, which was last week. We've been going out for nearly a year, so you'd think we'd have done it by now. But Cam's not like other boys.

I even had to talk Cam into having this party tonight. As soon as I heard his parents were going to London for the weekend I started working on him. It was the sex talk that broke him down, of course. I told him it'd be the first chance to do it after my birthday. He may be the perfect gentleman and everything, but he's still a *boy*.

Cam's so nervous about our first time. It's pretty sweet, really. I'm nervous too, but not for the same reasons as him. I'm worried he'll realise that this *isn't* my first time. Not even close.

I'm the worst girlfriend in the world.

At last Tilly lets me sit in front of the mirror. I try to get my boring hair to do something interesting, but in the end it just hangs there and looks brown. Sometimes I want to cut off all my hair and dye it like Tilly did last year. But I'd never be brave enough to do something like that. And I wouldn't want people to think I was ... like her.

I feel my face go red with shame, but Tilly's too busy fiddling with her nose ring to notice. But it's true. I wouldn't want people to think I'm gay. It's OK for Tilly – she's all cool and doesn't give a toss what anyone thinks. It's not like our school is full of gay kids or anything. There are maybe five or six kids who are 'out', and Tilly and Summer are the only girls.

I wasn't that surprised when Tilly told me she liked girls. It almost seemed like something I'd always known. It didn't change anything – not really. I'm always asking her if she fancies girls we see when we're out and about. And she always says no. But she's been acting weird for a while now. She's been distracted just like I am when there's a new boy I'm obsessed with. And now seems like the right time to nag her about it.

"So, Till," I say. "When are you going to tell me about this secret crush you've got?"

"I don't know what you're talking about." Tilly's busy doing up her Doc Martens, but she blushes bright red and that's when I know for sure.

"Is it Summer? I bet it's Summer! Come on, you can tell me."

Tilly sighs and rolls her eyes. "Just because Summer is the only other lesbian at school, it doesn't mean I fancy her!"

"I know, I know. I just thought she might be your type, that's all."

She looks up at me. "Since when do you know my *type*?"

I shrug. "I think Summer's pretty cool. A little scary, but cool ... You know she'll be there tonight, right?" I can't keep the cheeky grin off my face. "So ... all I'm saying is, tonight would be the perfect time to tell your secret crush how you feel ... Because *everyone's* going to be there. And there will be plenty of booze so you don't need to be shy."

I think I might have gone too far. Tilly looks well pissed off, but then she smiles. "You are so bloody annoying sometimes, Anna," she says. "You know that, right?"

I do know that. Still, it's not going to stop me from doing a little matchmaking at the party. Tilly just needs a little push in the right direction, that's all.

That's what best friends are for, right?

Chapter 2

Tilly gets annoyed with me on the bus to Cam's house. It's because I won't shut up about this secret crush of hers. I'm only doing it to keep my mind off what a terrible person I am.

I carry on until she gives me a warning look – a look that says I really, really should stop talking. Tilly's the sort of person who'll put up with a lot, but even *she* has a breaking point. Tonight that breaking point seems to be when I start wondering out loud if kissing a girl is all that different to kissing a boy.

"Anna, will you just shut up for one minute?!" Tilly says. "I *know* what you're doing. You're trying to distract yourself from how bad you feel about cheating on Cam. Well, I hope you feel better because you're making *me* feel crap."

"I'm sorry I'm sorry I'm sorry," I say in the most pathetic voice I can. I lean my head against hers and stare out of the window. "I don't want you to be lonely, that's all. You know I just want you to be happy, right?"

Tilly doesn't call me a patronising cow, which is nice of her. "I know," she says.

I decide to push my luck, because that's the kind of person I am. "Just promise me that you'll at least talk to Summer at the party," I say. "You never know – she might even like you back."

Tilly's silent for a moment or two, but then she sighs. "Fine," she says. "You win."

I snuggle into her. "Excellent ... we can go on double dates and everything."

She elbows me in the side. Fair enough.

The ten-minute walk from the bus stop to Cam's house leaves me sweating. It said on the

web that it's the hottest day of the year so far.
So it's just as well this is a pool party.

I knock on the front door even though the
music inside is way too loud for anyone to hear
me. Cam had asked me to come round early to
help set up, but there was no way I was playing
the little housewife. Besides, I wanted to get
ready with Tilly. Getting ready is always the
best part of the night anyway. At that point
there's possibility. Nothing's been ruined yet.

Tilly hasn't been to Cam's house before. She
gazes at the pillars on either side of the front
door. "Bloody hell, Anna. You didn't tell me he
lived in a palace!" She's taking the piss – but not
much. Cam's place is more like a mansion than a
house. It always reminds me of the White House.
Cam's parents are proper rich, but you'd never
know it from talking to him – it embarrasses him
more than anything.

"You get used to it after a while, I promise."
This is a lie. I never get used to the fact that
there are *two* sets of stairs and the kitchen is

big enough to have a sofa in it as well as a table that's long enough for about twenty people. And I never get used to the fact that there's a swimming pool. Who has a *swimming pool* in Scotland? It's only warm enough to sunbathe three times a year, max. Still, today I'm not complaining. Sweat is trickling down my back and probably soaking the back of my bikini bottoms under my skirt.

Tilly's wearing her favourite pair of jeans – her only nod to the heat is the black vest she's wearing. She refused to wear a bikini or any type of swimwear. She hates showing off her body.

Inside the house, all the furniture has been pushed back to the walls. The fancy Chinese rugs must have been stashed in the attic and there's no sign of anything that could get broken. It's clear Cam didn't need my help setting up at all. When Tilly and I wander into the kitchen we find him standing behind the kitchen island. He's shaking a cocktail shaker and looking a bit daft. There's a row of bottles in front of him – spirits and mixers. If Cam was a normal person he would have raided his parents' drinks cabinet. That's what I would have done, but I know for a fact that he used the money he's saved up from his Saturday job to buy the drinks. He even asked his parents if it was OK to have a party ... and they said yes!

Cam's wearing a white vest, grey board shorts and flip-flops. His messy blond hair and tan almost make him look like a surfer. But I know for a fact that he tried surfing on holiday last year and was totally rubbish at it. And the tan is left over from his holiday in Thailand last month.

Cam smiles a huge smile when he sees me and Tilly. He rushes over and gives me a quick kiss and a long hug. "You're here. At last. I missed you," he whispers in my ear. I roll my eyes but no one sees. We only saw each other three days ago. Cam hugs Tilly next and tells her she looks good. Tilly blushes and looks awkward because she has no idea how to take a compliment.

Cam puts one arm round me and one round Tilly and steers us out to the deck at the back of the house. The house is on a steep hill, so there are steps down from the deck to the pool and garden. It's only just starting to get dark, but when we peer over the edge of the deck into the garden, the place looks magical. There are twinkly fairy lights on all the trees and little Chinese lanterns everywhere.

"Oh my God, Cam!" I say. "It looks amazing!"

Cam grins and gives me a little squeeze. "I hoped you'd like it."

"I *love* it! This must have taken all day." And all of a sudden I feel bad that I wasn't here to help.

Cam shrugs. "Nah, I did most of it last night."

Last night. When I was kissing a total stranger. I can tell Tilly's thinking the same thing – I can feel the weight of her gaze on me.

It doesn't feel good.

Chapter 3

By 9pm the party is in full swing. The music's even louder, but Cam's not worried because even the nearest neighbour is too far away to hear the racket. It's still pretty hot so most people are outside.

A group of boys from the year above have taken over the deep end of the pool. They're taking it in turns to see who can make the biggest splash off the diving board. So predictable. A group of girls sit on the edge of the pool, giggling and being pathetic. Also predictable.

I lean against Cam on a sun lounger. I'm feeling tipsy in a very nice way. Tilly's on the next lounger, and she's a bit too quiet. At first I think she might still be feeling sorry for Cam, but then I catch her looking over to where Summer's just appeared.

Summer is strolling over to join the boys at the deep end of the pool. Her scraggy denim shorts are slung so low I'm surprised we can't see her ass crack. She has a massive tattoo on her back. It's hard to tell what it is from here, but I'd guess it's a dragon. She's wearing a bikini top that looks like a bra and her boobs are way bigger than you'd think.

Summer starts joking around with the boys and I check out of the corner of my eye to see if Tilly's still watching her. She is. She has no idea I've caught her perving.

Cam starts to stroke my arm with a touch like a feather. It tickles and it's kind of distracting. The boys in the pool are chanting at Summer – "Do it, do it, do it." She smirks at them, turns and walks away from the pool. One of the boys shouts "LAME!" and Summer turns round and starts to run back to the pool at full speed. She leaps onto the diving board with ridiculous grace, takes another huge jump and sails over the heads of the boys. She curls up into a ball and lands with the biggest splash you could imagine. A wave of water crashes over the girls on the edge of the pool and they scream as the boys laugh and whoop and holler.

Cam laughs too loud in my ear. Tilly smiles as Summer appears out of the water at the shallow end and shakes her head like a wet dog. I don't laugh or smile, and I'm not sure why. Normally I'd be glad to see someone humiliate those idiot girls in public.

Then Tilly catches me watching her and her smile fades away to nothing. Neither of us speaks for a moment or two. I have the weirdest feeling in the pit of my stomach. It feels like ... loss.

Chapter 4

Cam's saying something. I try to tune back in but I can't tear my eyes away from Tilly. She looks different tonight but I can't put my finger on *how*. I put it down to the glow of the fairy lights. Or maybe it's the three cocktails I've had. (Cam tried to get me to stop at two, but that just made me down the third one even faster.)

I sit up too fast, which startles Cam and makes him spill his beer.

"Were you even listening to a word I said?" he asks. I turn to look at him. He's not angry. I would be if it was so obvious someone was ignoring me.

I stand up and look from Cam to Tilly and back again, so fast it almost makes me dizzy. They look up at me as if I'm being weird.

"Cam, I have to talk to Tilly. Would you mind ...?" I flap my hands to shoo him away, like he's an annoying fly I want to get rid of.

Cam sits very still for a moment or two and I think that maybe this is it. Maybe he's going to act like a regular human being at last and lose his temper.

Nope. He isn't.

"Sure," he says. "No worries. I'll just go and make sure no one's trashing the house."

I sit back down on the lounger and Tilly shakes her head. "I have no idea why he puts up with you," she says. "It's like he came from the Perfect Boyfriend factory or something and you ..."

"And I *what?*" There's a challenge in my voice.

"I dunno," she says. "It's like everyone sees you two as this perfect couple. And I suppose you sort of *are*. But sometimes I think you deserve better … Both of you." Tilly is peeling the label off her bottle of Corona and she won't look me in the eye.

I'm annoyed. I can't help it. If anyone's going to tell the truth about my relationship I'd like it to be *me*, thank you very much. "What are you talking about?" I demand. "Cam and I are happy together."

Tilly snorts. "Yeah, so happy you had your tongue down some random's throat last night."

"That was a mistake!" I howl. "I told you! God, I can't believe you're throwing that in my face right now." I get up and walk off – a bit unsteady on my feet – to the bottom of the garden. It's darker there.

Tilly follows me. Of course she does. "Anna, I'm sorry," she says. "I didn't mean it. I just want you to be happy, that's all."

Even in the dark, I can see her worried face. "Hey!" I say. "That's *my* line, remember?" I can't stay cross with Tilly – ever. "Come here, you," I say. We hug. Then I grab her hand and drag her back towards the pool.

"So ... I've decided something," I say.

Tilly says a suspicious sort of, "Yesssss?"

"I'm going to speak to Summer for you," I tell her. "And there's nothing you can do or say to change my mind. So there." And before she can say anything, I run. Fast as I can.

"Anna? Anna! Don't you dare! ANNA!" Tilly sounds a bit frantic and for a millisecond I wonder if I'm doing the right thing. But it's for her own good. She'll thank me later.

I spy Summer up ahead. She's leaning against a tree, smoking. You can tell she thinks she looks pretty cool. In fact, she *does* look pretty cool, but smoking is gross. She'll have to stop if she's going to be Tilly's new girlfriend.

I slow my run to a walk and Tilly catches up with me. She grabs my arm.

"Anna!" she pleads again.

I shake her off. "You coming with me, Till?" I ask. My grin fades when I see how furious she is.

Tilly shakes her head. "I hate you."

"Nah! You love me, really," I tell her. "Now get lost so I can do my matchmaking in peace." I kiss her cheek, ruffle her hair and give her a gentle shove.

Tilly breathes hard, her hands on her hips. "If you do this ..."

"What? You'll thank me for the rest of your life?"

"Piss off." There's no power behind her words. She just sounds tired. Defeated. She doesn't storm off, which is what I would have done. She just shakes her head and walks away.

I turn to the task at hand and walk right up to Summer. She watches me approach with an amused smile. Somehow I'd never noticed how tall she is before. She makes me kind of nervous, actually. Her black hair is still wet from the pool, and it's slicked back from her face. You'd expect someone with a name like Summer to be small and blonde and smiley, but she's none of those things.

"Can I help you?" she says. The question is somewhere in the middle between friendly and unfriendly.

"Hi!" I say. "I'm Anna. You're Summer, right?" She nods and I stick out my hand to shake hands with her before I realise I look like a moron. Summer looks at my hand, raises an eyebrow and does a half-smile.

"That's me," she drawls.

"That jump into the pool was pretty epic," I babble. "I bet those girls are ransacking the house right now in a frantic search for hair straighteners." I laugh and it sounds forced.

Summer says nothing.

"So ... anyway. This is a bit embarrassing, but I was wondering ... do you have a girlfriend?"

Summer smirks. "I thought you were going out with Cam? Or is that just a cover story for your top-secret lesbian life?"

"What?! No!" I can feel myself start to blush. "Um ... I'm straight," I say. "Totally."

"Everyone's straight until they're not," she says with a grin.

It takes me a second to figure out what that means. "Ha! Clever."

Summer looks at me like she thinks I'm the stupidest person on the planet. "In answer to your question, no, I don't have a girlfriend right now. Let me guess, you're asking for your baby dyke friend. The one who wasn't looking so happy with you a minute ago?"

"Er ... yeah," I say. "That's Tilly. She kind of likes you, I guess."

Summer takes a drag of her cigarette and blows the smoke out of her nostrils. So gross. "Hmm," she says. "And she couldn't tell me herself because ...?"

"She's shy. And kind of new to the whole 'being gay' thing."

Summer pierces me with a look. "And you're sure she likes *me*?"

There's something weird about the weight she puts on the word 'me' but I ignore it because things are going pretty well. "Yup," I say. "Do you think you might ...?"

She shrugs. "Get her to come see me later," she says.

I clap my hands together in the lamest way you can imagine before I remember that Summer is too cool for school. Then I nod. "Yeah. Will do. Er ... bye."

I feel very pleased with myself as I walk away.

Job done.

Now to find Tilly and tell her the good news.

Chapter 5

People are dancing in the living room. I've never seen real people dancing at a house party before. I thought it only happened in America or on TV. The music is pretty bad – I'm sure it's Cam's choice. He has terrible taste in music. It's pretty much his only flaw, and not one you can really use as an excuse for having kissed someone else.

Cam's up there dancing, but he doesn't dance like the others – he dances like he's alone in his bedroom. There's nothing awkward about him whatsoever. If it was anyone else, people might laugh and take the piss. But since it's Cam, people start to dance just as crazily, trying to out-do each other with mad moves.

Cam spots me as I scan the room looking for Tilly. His grin is so huge it almost breaks my heart. He bounds over and bows. "May I have this dance?"

I want to find Tilly as soon as possible, but Cam's being too adorable for words and just then a decent song comes on. I take his hand and we head to the middle of the room.

At first *I* feel awkward and look around to see who might be watching. But I soon loosen up and before long I'm dancing like an idiot. I'm sweating and my hair must be all over the place but I couldn't care less.

After a while a slow song comes on and Cam holds me close. I put my lips to his neck and he strokes my back. It feels good to be with him like this. Better than it's felt in ages. When the song ends, he looks into my eyes and mouths the words, "I love you." I do the same and it feels like the truth.

Later on, I can't find Tilly anywhere – it's almost like she's avoiding me or something. She'd better not have gone home without me.

At last I find her in the utility room, where she's sitting on the floor next to the tumble dryer. "There you are!" I say. "I thought you might have scarpered."

Tilly doesn't say anything. I kneel down in front of her on the cold tiled floor.

"Hey," I say gently. "What's up?" I *know* what's up, but I say it anyway.

Tilly leans her head back against the wall and I notice pencil markings and dates going up the wall. I look up and up until the markings stop – at about six foot, I'd guess. Cam's height.

"So. Just how badly did you embarrass me out there?" she asks. "Tell me the truth."

"Not even a little bit!" I protest. "I was really subtle about it. Summer only thought something was up because you ran off like that. Anyway, it doesn't even matter, because guess what? She likes you too! I am SO good at this matchmaking thing, I should set up my own website or something."

Tilly closes her eyes and I can see her jaw clench and unclench. "Great," she says. "Just great." Even *I* can tell that's sarcasm.

"Um ... the least you can do is thank me, Till," I say.

Tilly's eyes fly open. "Thank you? THANK YOU?! Are you kidding me? You expect me to be *grateful*? Jesus Christ, Anna. You are unbelievable." A tear trickles down her face and that's when I really know I've screwed up. Tilly never cries. She swipes at the tear, but another one appears in its place.

"Tilly? What ...? I don't understand ... I was doing you a favour. I knew you'd be too shy to talk to Summer yourself ... I just wanted to help."

"Well, thanks very much for your 'help'," she snaps. "But I'd appreciate it if you never 'helped' me again."

"But it's OK, Till! She *likes* you!" I reach for Tilly's hand but she jumps back like I've just given her an electric shock. "Tilly!" I say. "What the hell is *wrong* with you?"

"Don't touch me," she blurts. "Just ... don't. I can't let you touch me." She gets up and paces to the other side of the room. Cam's parents' utility room is as big as my bedroom at home so there's plenty of space for pacing.

I have no idea what's going on. Tilly and I have argued before – best friends argue all the time, don't they? But this seems different. A shiver runs through me in spite of the heat.

Tilly leans against the sink. I can't see her face because she's got her back to me. But I can tell she's crying from the way her shoulders are moving.

I get up and my knees crack, which usually makes Tilly giggle and call me an old woman. I go over and put my hand on her arm. I'm sure she'll shake it off, but she doesn't. "Talk to me, Tilly," I say. *"Please."*

"There's nothing to talk about." Her voice is thick with tears.

"Tilly, I'm sorry," I say. "I shouldn't have talked to Summer when you didn't want me to, but I swear I thought I was doing the right thing ... Anyway, now you two know you like each other, you can get on with it – you know, kissing and all that good stuff." I squeeze her arm so she knows I'm joking.

Tilly turns around and she looks so lost and sad that it breaks my heart. I'd do anything to make her feel better. I hug her hard, but it's like hugging a plank of wood. "Come on, Till," I say. "There's nothing to be embarrassed about. It's perfectly normal to fancy someone, you know."

Tilly looks into my eyes for the longest time and she's not crying any more. "I don't fancy her."

"Yes you do! I saw you checking her out earlier!"

"No. I wasn't." Tilly's eyes are begging me to believe her.

"Huh. No? You promise?"

"I promise." And now I do believe her. No wonder she's pissed off with me.

"Shit," I say. "I'm sorry, Till. It's no big deal though, right? I'll talk to Summer, clear things up. No harm done, yeah?"

"No harm done." But her words are hollow and her eyes tell the truth – harm has definitely been done.

"God, me and my big mouth," I gabble. "I don't know why you put up with me sometimes, I really don't. I'll try to be a bit less annoying in future, OK? Forgive me? Pleeeeeeease?" I grab Tilly round the waist and start to tickle her. It's the only sure-fire, guaranteed way to make her laugh. At first I think my efforts are going to fail for the first time ever, but Tilly's powerless in the face of my tickling tactics. She giggles and squirms and tries to escape. "I'm not stopping until you say you forgive me ..." I tell her. "Say it!"

"OK, OK, I surrender!" Tilly holds up her hands and backs away from me. "I forgive you ... but tickling's cheating and you know it. Come on, let's get back out there. Cam will be wondering where you've disappeared to."

We're both laughing now and it feels good. So normal and right. I suppose that's what makes me push my luck. I sling my arm around Tilly's neck as we head towards the door. I lean my head on hers. "So who is it, then? Who's this mystery girl of yours if it's not Summer?"

Tilly tenses up under my arm. "I thought you said you were going to be less annoying?"

"Aw, come on, Till! You can tell me. I promise I won't talk to her or do anything or interfere in any way at all."

"There's no mystery girl," she says. "There's no secret crush. Now can you please just leave it? Haven't you got big plans with Cam tonight?"

I lean against the door to block it. "Tell meeeeee! Just tell me who it is and I promise I won't say another word about it. I'll leave you in peace and I'll go and have sex with Cam."

And then something changes. I don't know what the look in her eyes means, but I know it scares me. It makes me wish I hadn't pushed her. But it's too late to take it back and we just stand there in silence.

"You really want to know who I like?" Her voice is lower than usual and each word is heavy somehow.

"Yes." But even I can hear that I don't sound so sure.

There's another long look between us and I realise what she's going to say a millisecond before she says it.

"It's you."

Chapter 6

It seems like we both stop breathing. Each of us waits for the other to say something, to do something. It's not going to be me – every sensible thought has disappeared from my mind.

"It's not *like*," Tilly says at last. "I ... um ... I'm in love with you." As soon as the words are out she slumps. Like the effort of saying them was just too much for her. "I'm sorry, Anna," she says. "I really am. I tried to ignore it – even tried to make myself fancy Summer if you can believe it. But it just won't go away, no matter what I do." She won't make eye contact with me now.

I'm still too scared to speak. I know she wants me to say something – anything – to reassure her, but it's like my mouth's been glued shut.

"Anna? Talk to me … Please. What are you thinking?" She looks at me with pleading eyes. But I still can't find the words.

She takes my hand and squeezes it. "You're my best friend, Anna. I don't want anything to change that. Let's just pretend I never said anything, OK? We can go back to normal and I promise you don't have to worry about me jumping on you or anything. I'll get over this – I just need a bit of time. I … I can't lose you, Anna. I can't."

I look down at my hand in hers and Tilly does the same. She says, "Sorry," and lets go of it. Her voice is so very small and I can't bear to hear her like this.

At last, my mouth comes unstuck. "There's nothing to apologise for," I say.

I lean towards her. Slowly, very slowly. And it feels like my heart might just push its way out of my chest. Tilly's eyes widen. They're impossibly blue this close up. I feel like I've never seen them this close up before, even though that can't be true.

Our lips meet in a perfect, gentle kiss.

Tilly's lips feel so different to Cam's – or any other boy I've kissed. They're soft – so very soft. My hand finds its way to the back of her head and I pull her closer to me. I open my mouth and the tip of my tongue meets hers and it's so much better than any kiss I've ever had in my life.

And then I realise I'm kissing Tilly, my best friend. I'm kissing a girl. I do not kiss girls. I kiss *boys*. I like *boys*. I pull my head back and sort of squirm away so I'm not pinned against the door. We're both breathing hard and I feel hot and cold and weird.

Tilly's eyes are filled with confusion. She reaches out to me, but I jerk away from her hand.

"Get away from me! Jesus Christ, Tilly! I'm not ... I like boys. You know that!"

"But you ... *you* kissed *me?!*"

I shake my head. I can't think straight. I *can't* have been the one to kiss her. It's not possible. I would never do something like that. "Just ... leave me alone, OK?" I say. "Don't ... This never happened."

"We need to talk about this, Anna. That kiss was ..." Her voice is gentle. She closes her eyes and leans towards me and I push her – hard enough to make her stumble backward. "What the hell?! Anna!"

"I'm not gay, OK! Get that into your stupid head!" Tears well up in my eyes like they always do when I'm angry.

Tilly's crying too, but I feel nothing. *She* did this. *She* made this happen. It's all her fault. "Please, Anna!" she pleads. "We can't leave things like this ..."

I take a deep breath and wipe away my tears. "I think it would be best if we gave each other some space." My voice sounds so cold and hard. But I have to go that little bit further, just to make my point. "Cam will be waiting."

"You're not still going to sleep with him?" Tilly asks in horror.

"That's *exactly* what I'm going to do."

We stand there and look at each other for a couple of seconds. I can tell Tilly's searching for a crack in my armour. Something to tell her I don't mean what I'm saying. She won't find it – I'll make sure of that.

I put my hand on the door handle and begin to turn it. I expect Tilly to stop me, to beg me to stay. But she doesn't.

I leave the room without a backwards glance.

Chapter 7

Cam. I need to find Cam. NOW.

He's upstairs on the balcony with those idiot boys from before. And Summer. They're all passing around a bottle of vodka and a joint, but Cam's sipping from a can of Coke. I know he's pacing himself because of what we've planned for later. The boys are lounging on some huge black and white cushions from Cam's room. Summer's leaning over the balcony and I have a sudden urge to grab her legs and tip her over the edge.

I grab the bottle from one of the lads and take a few big swigs. The vodka burns in my throat and my eyes start to water, but I manage not to choke. One of the boys says, "Easy, tiger!" and takes the bottle back.

"I'm telling you ... I could totally do it. It's not that far," Summer says. She turns away from the balcony's edge.

"Bullshit!"

"No way!"

"You're a crazy bitch."

I have no idea what they're on about.

Cam says nothing. He watches me, and I wonder if he's bothered by the way I gulped the vodka.

Summer slumps down on a cushion. "You boys are such pussies. You know that, right? It's, like, half the distance I jumped from the diving board."

Right. So she's talking about jumping from the balcony into the pool. She IS a crazy bitch. But if she wants to get her brains splattered all over the deck, I'm not going to stop her.

I want to get away from these people as soon as possible. "Cam, can I talk to you for a minute?" I ask.

Cam gets up and turns to Summer. "Don't do it. Just ... don't. I mean it." He sounds like a teacher.

Summer's got the vodka now and she downs it like it's water. "Whatever you say, Golden Boy." She turns to me. "Hey, where's your friend?"

"How the hell would I know?! We're not joined at the hip, you know!" The boys make annoying 'ooooh' sounds in chorus. I grab Cam's hand and lead him down the hall to his bedroom.

I lock the door behind us and sit on the edge of the bed. Cam sits next to me. "So what do you want to talk about? Are you OK, Anna? You seem a little ..."

"A little what?" I snap back.

"Stressed? Edgy? Weird? All of the above?" He puts his hand on my knee and laughs to show me I'm not supposed to be offended.

I just kissed my best friend. How the hell am I supposed to feel? "I'm fine, Cam," I say. "Honest."

Cam sighs and lies back on the bed. "Glad to hear it," he says. "God, I'm knackered. Parties are a lot less stressful when they're at someone else's house."

"Yeah, but no one else has a swimming pool, do they?" I say. "It's pretty much your God-given duty to have a party in this place."

It's now or never. I straddle him in one swift move and his eyes widen in surprise.

He starts to say something but I cover his mouth with mine. For a second I wonder if my mouth tastes different to him. If he can tell I've been kissing someone else. But that's insane.

Cam's not a bad kisser. Kissing him is more pleasant than doing lots of other things. I'd rather kiss him than learn my French vocab. I'd rather kiss him than watch those crappy antiques programmes Mum loves so much. I'd rather kiss him than kiss …

I try to relax into the kiss, to focus on his hands resting on my hips. It's working. I'm getting into this. Everything's going to be OK. My hands move down to the front of Cam's shorts.

Cam pulls away. "What are you …?"

"What does it look like I'm doing?!" I say. He looks towards the door. "Don't worry," I tell him. "It's locked."

"But … everyone's still here," he says, as I kiss his neck the way he usually kisses mine.

"Who cares?"

"Um … *I* do? You don't seriously expect me to be able to … you know … right now? What if someone hears? What if people trash the house? What if – "

My hand snakes inside his shorts, and that shuts him up. He starts to breathe hard and I know I've won. "God, that feels good." His voice is low and thick with lust. Boys are simple creatures.

A few minutes later Cam's on top of me. He's still wearing his shorts and I'm still wearing my bikini and my skirt, but I plan to do something about that ASAP. I like the way his back feels under my hands.

"Have you got any condoms?" I whisper in his ear, trying to make it sound sexy.

He clambers off me and starts to rummage in his bedside drawer. "They're here somewhere ... I could swear I put them just ..." He pulls out a box of Durex, then takes out one of the little foil wrappers. "Do you want me to turn the lights off ... or ...?"

I'm lying on my boyfriend's bed.

"Babe, do you want the lights on or off?" His voice seems very far away.

I'm going to have sex with my boyfriend.

"Anna? Are you sure you want to do this? We don't have to do this, you know. It's completely up to you. I'm happy to wait. You know that, right?"

My boyfriend is talking to me and I have no idea what to say to him.

His face looms over mine, worried. "Are you OK? Anna? Talk to me."

I don't want to be lying on my boyfriend's bed. I don't want to have sex with my boyfriend.

I sit up fast, like I've just woken up from a nightmare. I'm dizzy for a moment and then the feeling passes and all of a sudden everything's *clear*. I speak the words before I have time to think about them. They fall from my mouth so easily.

"I'm in love with Tilly."

Chapter 8

Cam's reaction isn't exactly what I expect. Even if I'd had a million guesses as to what his reaction might be, I don't think I'd have guessed right. He doesn't look angry or sad or confused. He looks like I've just told him that I like Nutella on my toast or I've just got a new phone. Neutral. That's the best word for it.

He scoots back up the bed to lean against the headboard. I do the same.

"Well? Aren't you going to say something?" I say.

"What would you like me to say?" His voice is as neutral as his face.

"I don't know!" I say. "Tell me what you feel! Tell me I'm the biggest bitch on the planet! Just … say *something*." I pause to look at him. Still neutral. "I just told you I'm in love with a girl, for Christ's sake!" I say. "Don't you have *anything* to say about that?"

I want him to say something. Anything. I need him to say something so I don't have to think about my words and what they might mean.

Cam takes my hand – another surprise. "I already knew, Anna." He says it gently, like he's trying really hard not to hurt my feelings. He sees that I'm about to argue so he rushes on. "OK, maybe I didn't know for sure. Not that you *love* her … but I knew there was something there with you two. At first I thought it was just that you've known each other forever and you're really close. But then I realised it's more than that."

"*When?!* When did you realise?" I feel like we're discussing something else now. Not the death of *us*. It's like we're talking about something which neither of us feel that strongly about.

"Tilly's birthday," he says.

'Two months ago?' I think. 'Two WHOLE months ago.'

"I'd started to notice things before then, I suppose," he goes on. "Like the fact that you're a different person when she's around. You're more *you*, if that makes sense. You have this different kind of energy, like you're buzzing or something." Cam shakes his head. "God, I'm not explaining this very well, am I?"

I shrug. "What was so special about Tilly's birthday?" I ask.

But *everything* had been special about Tilly's birthday – I'd made sure of it. Her parents never spoil her like mine spoil me and birthdays aren't a big deal in her house. So I made up my mind that was what her birthday would be – a big deal. The biggest deal. I'd spent ages saving up and tracking down the perfect present – a signed first edition of her favourite book. It had cost a fortune – I'd never spent that much money on anything before. Tilly cried when she opened it. Her hands shook and she kept saying, "I can't believe it," over and over again. She said it was the nicest thing anyone had ever done for her. It was this perfect, perfect moment. Except that Cam was there with his big arms wrapped around me.

I'd baked a cake too. In fact, I'd baked *two* cakes – the first one was a total disaster. It was carrot cake, even though I think the idea of a cake with carrot in it is the stupidest thing ever. Tilly ate three slices so I knew that the second cake had turned out OK.

"Um ... you got me an X-box game for *my* birthday," Cam says.

"But you love that game!"

He smiles, a little, sad smile. "I *do* love it. But you can see what I'm getting at, right? I'm not trying to be a dick about this. I just wish I'd realised how you felt before I fell for you, that's all. I wish *you'd* realised."

"I had no idea." And it's the truth. It's crazy – you can have no clue about something one minute, and then know it 100% the next minute, like magic. Or maybe it's just *my* brain that's so good at hiding the truth from me.

"I believe you," Cam says. He's not being sarky – Cam is *never* sarky. And it's important to me that he believes me. Even though I've lied to him so many times before, I didn't lie about this. I don't know why that fact is so important to me, but it is.

I have a sudden desire to snuggle up in his arms where things are safe and normal and not confusing. It would be so easy to pretend. But Cam *knows* and he deserves better. He could have any girl he wants but for some reason he chose me. I was a terrible girlfriend even before any of this Tilly stuff. And what exactly IS this Tilly stuff anyway? What the hell am I going to do now?

Cam gives me a little bump with his elbow. "Have you told her?"

I shake my head.

"You should, you know. Tonight."

"Why are you being so ... cool about this?" I ask. "You must hate me." Part of me *wants* him to hate me. I deserve it.

Cam sighs. "I don't know. It's kind of a relief, I suppose. I don't want you to be with me when you want to be with someone else. You should have a chance to be happy. Everyone should. I could never hate you, Anna. Never. You know how I feel about you. It's not your fault you don't feel the same way – you can't help who you love."

"I'm sorry, Cam," I say. "I'm so sorry. I wish ..." I don't know what I wish so I stop talking.

"I know," he says. He gets up from the bed and holds out his hand to me. He helps me up from the bed. There's nothing else to be done.

One of us has to make a move to leave the room and I know it should be me.

"Can I get a hug, please?" I have no right to ask for anything from him, but he nods and takes me in his arms.

"I'm not sure I can do this. I'm not sure I want to be ..." I whisper and my lips brush against his neck.

"Gay?" Cam pulls away a little so he can look at me. He laughs. I wasn't expecting that. "Who cares?!" he says. "It's not like you have to decide now, anyway. Maybe you're gay, maybe you're not. Maybe it's about falling in love with a *person*, you know?"

I can't believe how badly I have treated this boy. This loving, understanding boy.

"Do you really believe that?" I ask.

He looks at me in that intense way of his. I used to think that look was the sexiest thing on the planet. "The only thing that matters is what *you* believe, Anna," he says. It sounds like a line from a cheesy movie, but I can tell he really means it. Then he gives me a little shove. "Now go and find Tilly and tell her how you feel."

I take a deep breath and let it out slowly. "OK. Right. Yes. Are you sure you're OK?"

"I'm fine, I promise! Now get out of here before I change my mind!"

When I leave the room Cam's sitting on the end of the bed.

He doesn't look very OK.

Chapter 9

I close the door behind me and it's like closing the door on a huge part of my life. What happens next is completely up to me. It scares me.

I stop in front of the mirror in the hall. My hair's a mess. I try to pat it down to make it look like I haven't been rolling around in Cam's bed. Then I turn and follow the noise on the balcony. The boys are still there with Summer and they're chanting, "Jump! Jump! Jump!" It's clear they're not going to give up until someone takes a dive into that pool.

One of the boys moves out of the way and I see her. Tilly. She has a bottle of tequila in her hand even though she's never drunk tequila in her whole life. She sees me at exactly the same moment I see her. I smile but she doesn't smile back. She takes a swig of tequila without breaking eye contact with me.

Everything after this happens very fast – and somehow it's all very slow at the same time. That's the only way I can explain it.

I hear a sound behind me and I feel a hand on my arm. A friendly squeeze from Cam to reassure me. Tilly looks away fast and I realise what she must think. She thinks I've had sex with Cam. Shit.

I have to explain. I have to tell her everything. I take a few steps towards the balcony but stop when Tilly slings her arm around Summer. The way she does it is so easy – so casual – like it's something she does every day. Like *they're* the ones who are best friends. I wonder how much I missed when I was in Cam's room. Maybe I'm too late. Maybe Tilly does like Summer after all. Maybe she lied to me.

Tilly whispers something in Summer's ear which makes her eyes light up. Her hand is resting on Tilly's hip; I want to smash that stupid hand with a hammer. But unfortunately I don't have a hammer.

Tilly glances over to check I'm watching then she plants a kiss on Summer's lips. I don't know who's more surprised – Summer or the boys. Or me.

I'm dimly aware of Cam standing next to me, watching this little nightmare unfold. He puts his arm around me which is exactly the wrong thing to do. It's like some horrible mirror image – Tilly with her arm around Summer and Cam with his arm around me. Why do we have our arms around the wrong people?

Then everything gets crazy. Tilly climbs onto a chair and she's swaying a bit. She puts her hand on Summer's shoulder to steady herself, then she looks over the edge of the balcony. And somehow I know what she's thinking, even though it's the most un-Tilly thing you could imagine.

That stupid chant starts up and Summer joins in. Cam's saying something like, "Stop it now. Can everyone just go downstairs?" His voice sounds like pure panic.

Then it's like everyone disappears and there's just me and Tilly. I'm standing maybe three metres away from her but it might as well be three miles. My voice comes out cracked and broken and I'm not even sure that it's loud enough for her to hear. "Get down from there, Tilly. Don't be stupid."

They were the wrong words. I wanted to say, 'Tilly, I love you. I'm sorry and I love you and I didn't have sex with Cam so there's nothing to worry about.' That's what I *should* have said.

Tilly shakes her head and takes one more massive gulp of tequila. She passes the bottle to Summer and says, "Here, hold this." Summer is looking up at her like she's the coolest thing on the planet.

Tilly hitches up her jeans and puts one foot up on the railing. I can see her take a deep breath and I'm running as fast as I can towards her. Cam is one step ahead of me and he's shouting, "No!" and I'm shouting the same thing at the same time. The chanting suddenly stops like someone flicked a switch.

She doesn't jump – she *dives*. She disappears from view and my heart plummets with her.

Chapter 10

I hear a splash, which is exactly what I wanted to hear. She's made it into the pool.

But then I hear screams from below.

Cam and I reach the railing at the same time.

I see Tilly in the pool. That's exactly what I hoped I'd see. But she's face down and there's redness billowing out into the water from her head.

People are standing round the pool, sobbing and screaming. Why isn't anyone *doing* anything? I'm about to ask Cam but he's clambering over the railing and he jumps before I can say anything. I check that he's landed OK before I shove Summer out of the way and race downstairs. By the time I get outside Cam is climbing up the steps of the pool with Tilly in his arms. There's blood where her head touches his shoulder. She looks like a ragdoll.

"She's not breathing," Cam says.

It's my fault. I did this. I DID THIS.

Cam gives her mouth-to-mouth. Somehow he knows just what to do. I watch her chest rise and fall, rise and fall as he forces air into her lungs. He keeps going the whole time we wait for the ambulance. He doesn't give up. He would never give up.

I'm aware of girls crying somewhere in the background.

I'm aware of Summer asking me again and again, "Do you think she'll be OK?"

I'm aware of one of those idiot boys saying, "We didn't think anyone would actually do it. We were just messing around." As if that makes any difference.

I'm aware that my best friend, the girl I love, is very possibly dying in front of my eyes.

The ambulance arrives. And the police. Summer's nowhere to be seen.

Cam hugs me and helps me into the ambulance. It's too hot inside.

I sit next to Tilly while the paramedics work on her. They tell me they're trying to stabilise her.

There are splashes of blood on the floor. It looks too red – like fake horror-movie blood. A stupid thought pops into my head.

I wish Tilly was here with me.

I grab her hand and hold it up to my mouth. Her hand feels wet and cold and lifeless on my lips. I try to squeeze some warmth into it.

Please don't die. Please don't die. Please don't die.

If I say it enough times in my head, maybe it will save her. But how many times will be enough? She's running out of time. I can see it in their eyes.

"Can I ... talk to her?" I ask.

The male paramedic with the kind face nods. "Sure," he says. "Won't do any harm." The female paramedic with the blonde hair looks at me like she knows this is my fault. Somehow she *knows*.

I don't care what she thinks. I don't care what *anyone* thinks. I just need to speak to Tilly. I need to say the words I wanted to say when I came out of Cam's room. Even if I'm not sure she can hear them.

"I love you, Tilly." I whisper it. Then I say it louder. Again and again. I love you, Tilly.

The monitor Tilly's hooked up to makes an angry beeping sound and the woman's forehead creases up with worry. The paramedics both work faster now. Something's happening. Something not good is happening.

Tilly can't die.

She just *can't*.

Tilly is a good person. She's never hurt anyone in her whole life. She deserves to live a long and happy life. The world would be a worse place without Tilly in it. Bad things shouldn't happen to good people like her. That's not how things are supposed to work.

I am a *bad* person. I've hurt Cam and Tilly. Perhaps this is the punishment you get for being a bad person. Someone you love gets hurt so you learn not to be so horrible. You learn to treat people better and be kind to animals and help old ladies across the street. If that's it, then I've learned my lesson. I *will* be a better person. I promise. There's no need for Tilly to die.

I would give anything to turn back the clock a few hours. Just one chance to make things right. That's all it would take. Tilly and I would be back in my room getting ready for the party. But this time I wouldn't tease her about that secret crush. This time I would look in Tilly's eyes and see how she feels about me. And I would tell her that I feel the same way. We wouldn't even go to Cam's house. Tilly would never see the balcony, let alone jump off it. The two of us would stay together and everything would be fine. We might even live happily ever after.

Tilly can't die. Not now. Not like this.

Everything is still. The male paramedic with the kind face has his hand on my shoulder and he's saying some words but I can't seem to understand them. "Anna? *Anna?* Are you listening to me?" I look at him. Then I look at the woman with the blonde hair. They both have the same expression on their face and at first I can't work out what it is. But then I see. Pity. It's pity.

"Anna? She's gone."

She's *gone*.

LE	10/13